THIS TIME IS TROUBLE

Grimalkin Academy
Book 6

LAURA GREENWOOD

© 2021 Laura Greenwood

All rights reserved. This book or parts thereof may not be reproduced in any form, stored in any retrieval system, or transmitted in any form by any means – electronic, mechanical, photocopy, recording or otherwise – without prior written permission of the published, except as provided by United States of America copyright law. For permission requests, write to the publisher at "Attention: Permissions Coordinator," at the email address; lauragreenwood@authorlauragreenwood.co.uk.

Visit Laura Greenwood's website at:

www.authorlauragreenwood.co.uk

Cover by Vampari Designs

This Time Is Trouble is a work of fiction. Names, characters, places, and incidents are the products of the author's imagination or are used fictitiously. Any resemblance to actual persons, living or dead, businesses, companies, events, or locales is entirely coincidental.

If you find an error, you can report it via my website. Please note that my books are written in British English: https://books.authorlauragreenwood.co.uk/errorreport

To keep up to date with new releases, sales, and other updates, you can join my mailing list via my website or my Reader Group on Facebook.

Mona, Ryan, and Rhubarb are causing havoc on the dig of their dreams.

Now her curse is lifted, Mona has a chance to follow her dream of becoming an archaeologist. When a chance to take part in one comes up, she can't refuse, even if it means leaving her kittens, Caspian, and Thomas behind for a few weeks.

Everything is going to plan until Mona and Ryan find themselves lost in a tomb and in need of a kitten to come to the rescue.

Luckily for them, Rhubarb has come along for the ride.

-

This Time Is Trouble is book six of Grimalkin Academy, and is a HEA story for Mona, an urban fantasy academy series featuring two best friends, lots of kittens, and a low-heat poly romantic subplot.

If you enjoy paranormal academy, cute familiars, light-hearted romance, witches, and friendship, you should start the Grimalkin Academy series today.

Chapter 1

"How did you arrange this?" I ask Thomas as he slips his hand into mine.

"I have friends in high places," he says, wiggling his eyebrows.

I snort, but go with it. I love watching the sharks, and being able to do it when no one else is around is a definite plus. He guides me through the rooms, and we stop and stare at some of the fish as we do. With only the workers around, we can spend as long as we want looking at them all.

The large tank full of huge sharks and turtles rising up in front of us, and it's all I can do not to run towards it and press my hands up against the glass and stare in at the fish.

This is supposed to be a romantic date, not me acting like a five-year-old seeing big fish for the first time.

"You'll want to come down to the tunnel," Thomas says.

I cock my head to the side and look back at him. "Why?"

"You'll see." A teasing glint enters his eyes.

What's he up to? I haven't seen him this secretive since...well, ever. He wasn't even like this when we were running around and doing black magic behind everyone's backs. Well, not everyone. Caspian, Ryan, and Daphne were all in on it too, but we're the only ones. Hopefully, no one will ever find out about it.

He guides me past the huge tank window. A pang of regret fills me as we move away, but then I remember we're on our own here, and I can simply come back after Thomas' surprise is over.

Light dances on the wall, the reflections of the water rippling across it. Faint music comes from the tunnel. I frown, then flash another look at Thomas. What's he up to?

"Go on," he urges.

I step into the tunnel and marvel at the set up in front of me. "We're having a picnic?" I ask, though the answer is evident. There's a blanket and pillows stretched out in the middle of the tunnel, and a hamper sat by it. The music is coming from a set of tiny speakers next to it.

"You keep saying you never have enough time to enjoy the tunnel when we come. So I thought we'd have a whole meal of it," Thomas says.

A large smile stretches over my face. The aquarium is far enough away from Grimalkin that I don't think anyone has ever noticed I come with a teaching assistant, but even so, we like to be careful. Given our 'service to the academy', I doubt there'd be any consequences from them finding out about it, but it's better to be safe than sorry.

"It's wonderful, thank you."

I ignore the fish for a moment, even though it's hard, and make my way to Thomas. I wrap my arms around his neck and pull him in for a kiss. He returns it within moments, and I melt into his arms. While it's fun to hang out with all three of my boyfriends at once, I cherish the one on one time I can spend with them.

Thomas breaks the kiss after another moment. "I thought about inviting the others, but then I decided I wanted some alone time with you before you jet off halfway around the world."

I flash him an easy smile, hopefully reassuring him that I don't plan on forgetting any of them any time soon. "I'll still be able to video call," I point out, though secretly I'm glad to be able to spend some time with him, and hopefully with Caspian, before Ryan and I leave for the dig.

"You chose right. I think Caspian wants to take me on a date on Thursday."

"Yes, he mentioned something like that." Thomas directs me to the blanket, and I drop myself down onto it, leaning against one of the pillows and staring up at the fish as they swim overhead.

One of the sharks passes over us, his body swaying back and forth with an elegance that can't be denied.

"Did you know sharks have a sixth sense?" Thomas asks.

I laugh softly. "Yes. It's to do with sensing the electrical fields that other animals make."

"Well, there goes any chance I have of impressing you," Thomas jokes.

"You know that's not the case." I sit up and place a hand against his back in what I hope is a reassuring gesture. "You've already impressed me, you don't have to do it again."

"Mona, I'm never going to stop trying to impress you. I love you. Your happiness is the most important thing in the world to me."

My heart flutters hearing the words, even though I have countless times. "I love you too," I reply. "But your own should be just as important," I remind him. It's a conversation we have regularly. Mostly because he's a workaholic and sometimes needs reminding he can do things for fun. I hope I've been good for him on that front.

"I know."

A hammerhead shark swims past, reminding me of his shark fact. "Did you know that hammerheads have the best sixth sense of all the sharks?" I try.

He chuckles. "I might have seen that when

I was looking up facts to impress you with. They have three-sixty vision too."

Another one joins the first, as if called here by the subject of our conversation. We lapse into comfortable silence as we watch the fish swim around above us. It's beautiful, and peaceful. Like nothing I've ever experienced before. He's going to have to get a private viewing of the aquarium for us again at some point.

"Meow."

Oh no. I'd recognise that sound anywhere.

The two of us exchange a knowing glance before turning our attention to the picnic basket.

"Did you..." I start.

Thomas flips open the lid of the picnic basket, and a small furry striped head pops out of it and looks around.

I sigh. "He is impossible." It doesn't take a genius to work out that Rhubarb has been up to his usual mischief, and that Thomas had no idea the kitten was there.

I scoop him out of the basket and set him down on the blanket.

"If you've eaten our dinner, Rhubarb, I'm

going to be cross," I threaten, waggling my finger at the kitten and not meaning a word of it. How can I be mad at him when he's so cute?

"I should have known better than to try leaving him in your room," Thomas mutters.

"You really should." I kiss him on the cheek so he knows I don't blame him for the kitten's misbehaviour. No one is to blame for that except Rhubarb himself, the sneaky kitty.

Thomas unpacks the picnic, spreading the food out around us. After pulling out a thermos, he hands me a mug of tea. I clasp my hands around it and blow across the top. This date can't possibly get any better. Privacy, hundreds of square metres of water above our heads, and tea. Perfection.

Rhubarb seems to have found his feet again and heads off in the direction of the tank. It takes him a couple of attempts, but he manages to balance himself on the small ledge next to the glass. He bats it with his paw as a dark fish with whiskers coming from its face. The two creatures stare at one another.

"Is he in a staring match with a catfish?" Thomas asks.

"I think so." I smother a laugh. This is right up there in the list of silly things Rhubarb has done.

Thomas settles back onto the pillows, then pulls me into him to watch the fish and the kitten.

"How long have we got here?" I ask.

"Until ten." He kisses the side of my head.

I relax further into him. "Good."

This is perfect. One of my boyfriends, fish swimming overhead, and even one of my kittens.

Life really is perfect.

Chapter 2

"It's so hot and dusty," Ryan shouts over the rumbling of the jeep as it travels over the desert.

I chuckle to myself. I'm not sure why he's so surprised by that. We're in Egypt, of course it's going to be hot and dusty. It doesn't stop this being an opportunity of a lifetime. Neither does the fact I'm missing the others. I'm sure Thomas and Caspian would have come with us if they could, but by the time Daphne and her boyfriends tagged along, it'd be too many people. Besides, someone needs to look after the kittens.

Which leaves just me and Ryan.

I reach out for his hand and entwine our

fingers. It's so comfortable to show him affection now. Though I suppose no one will think anything of it here. With only him in tow, I don't have to explain the three boyfriends thing. In theory. I'm sure it'll come up at some point.

The jeep comes to a rumbling halt as it nears a group of tents all pitched neatly in a row.

My heart leaps with excitement. I can't believe we're here. It seems like so long ago that the two of us applied for work experience on the dig site, and even then, it seemed like a long shot that we'd both get picked. So many people apply. But after my curse was vanquished, we all worked hard to get good grades so we can make the most of our education.

Ryan pulls away from me and jumps out of the car. He turns back to face me, a large grin on his face and an outstretched arm ready to help me down.

I roll my eyes. He knows I'm perfectly capable of getting in and out of vehicles on my own. But despite that, a small part of me still thinks it's a sweet gesture.

I let him catch me, then find my balance on the uneven and rocky ground.

A dark-haired woman with a long dark plait strides towards us. I don't want to stereotype, but she's exactly what everyone expects an archaeologist to look like. I suppose it's because there's some truth in it. I mean, I'm wearing the same kind of khaki and beige clothing as she is, and my hair is tied back and out of the way, though it doesn't stop a few stray strands from drifting over my face in the slight breeze.

And, to make matters worse, there wasn't anything I could do to dissuade Ryan from buying an Indiana Jones hat. I have to admit he looks cute in it.

"You must be the new interns," the woman says.

I nod. "I'm Mona Black, this is Ryan Chambers." I gesture to him as I introduce us.

"Good. I'm Doctor Bell. But you can call me Sabine."

I smile at her, but don't say anything, mostly because I'm not sure she wants me to.

"Grab your bags and follow me," she instructs.

We turn back to the jeep and unload the two huge bags we've packed with everything we might need. Plus a little extra. Our mums were fretting about us and wanted to make sure we had enough stuff. I swear half of my backpack is full of sunscreen. Apparently, they forgot that both Ryan and I are competent magic users and played a part in breaking a curse far above our supposed level already. If we forget sunscreen, we can just cast a spell and stop ourselves from burning.

We follow Sabine away from the car and towards a small tent in the middle of the camp. There are others of a similar size dotted around, as well as a much bigger one that must be used for camp meetings.

"This is yours. I'm sorry, you're going to have to share." She grimaces as if that's news she didn't want to give.

"It's not a problem," I assure her. "We've been dating for years."

Her eyebrows knit together as she takes me in. "I thought Mr Smith said you were his partner?" she prompts.

Oops. Perhaps I'm about to have the conversation the moment after arriving then.

Should have checked with Thomas about what he's told her. While I don't think his word is the main reason the two of us got picked for the internships, I don't think it hurt.

"I am. Ryan is also my boyfriend."

"She has a third one back home, too," Ryan puts in, grinning like this is the most amusing thing he's ever done. He loves seeing the expression on people's faces when they learn about my romantic situation. It would be annoying if he wasn't so cute.

"I assure you, Mr Smith is well aware of the situation," I promise, hoping to put any gossip to bed before it spreads around the camp.

Sabine sighs. "I don't care what you do with your private life, Miss Black. Just make sure there's no drama on my dig site."

"Absolutely," I respond instantly.

"The drama's all in our past," Ryan mutters under his breath.

I elbow him in the side. No one needs to know about the black magic, jailbreaks, and kitten making. That's all in the past now. In theory, anyway. A small part of me is waiting for Clan McIver to turn up again and take their revenge on us for uncovering their plot. Not that it was a very good one in the first place. I still don't understand why they let things happen the way they did.

Sabine's gaze flits between the two of us. "Just don't cause any problems. You'll be shadowing the main team at dig site two. Keep your heads down and do what your team leader says. If you don't cause any problems, then your names will be included in the official dig reports."

I perk up. "They will?"

She raises an eyebrow. "Isn't that why you came?"

"I came for the experience. No one takes a prospective archaeologist without it," I point out.

"Hmm. True." She nods. "Mr Smith mentioned that you're particularly good with breaking curses?"

My cheeks flush. "I mean..."

"She's the best in the class, along with my sister," Ryan supplies. "She's good at potions too."

"There isn't much call for potion-making

around here, but curse-breaking is another matter."

"It's what I want to go into," I mumble.

A thoughtful expression crosses her face. "I'll keep that in mind. But for now, unpack. Dinner is in the main tent in an hour and you'll start tomorrow."

She doesn't wait for us to respond and turns to walk away. I hope there's nothing else we need to know between now and dinner, though I doubt it.

"After you," Ryan says, gesturing towards the empty tent that'll be our home for the next few weeks.

Hopefully, we don't drive one another crazy in that time.

Chapter 3

I try not to think about how much sand is going to get everywhere as I unpack the clothing we brought and place it in a trunk. I'm glad they've provided us with storage space. We haven't been able to bring that much with us and I'll need my rucksack for while we're out at the dig site to carry tools and water.

The chirping of my tablet pulls me away from my task.

"Your mum or mine?" I ask Ryan who is closer to it.

He frowns. "Daphne."

Huh. I'm not expecting a call from my best

friend yet. We've already sent one another messages, like always. But I miss her. We haven't spent that much time apart in the past few years between living in the same flat and me spending part of the holidays with her and Ryan.

"Answer it?"

He does, and the familiar pink-haired witch appears on the screen with Caspian and Thomas on either side of her.

My heart lifts at the sight of them and I realise how much I've missed them all.

Already.

This doesn't bode well for surviving the next few weeks without getting unbelievably homesick. Though as of tomorrow, I'll have plenty to distract me from mooning over my boyfriends and missing my best friend.

"Hey guys," Ryan says, waving at the camera awkwardly.

They return the gesture. I've no idea why we do it when none of us are uncomfortable around each other, but it seems to be the universal greeting of video chats.

"How was your flight?" Daphne asks.

"Fine. It wasn't even that long," I respond, coming over to sit by Ryan so we can all chat properly.

"And the jet lag?"

I chuckle. "We're only an hour ahead of you, I don't think jet lag is going to be much of a problem." Though if I do pursue this as a career, that will change. I doubt all of my digs will be in Egypt. And I hope they aren't. There are fascinating sites and history all around the world and I want to uncover it all.

"How are things on your end? Missing us yet?" Ryan asks.

Caspian rubs the back of his neck, a nervous expression crossing his face.

"Oh no, what's happened?" I ask. "Did someone get cursed?"

"Or worse, did one of the kittens disappear again?" Ryan adds.

Thomas and Caspian exchange a guilty look.

"Did you lose one of my kittens?" I ask, trying to keep calm. I had a bad feeling as I was saying goodbye to them but I ignored it. Now I know why.

"We can't find Rhubarb," Caspian admits.

"What?" I try to keep the shock out of my voice and the panic under control, but I don't think I'm doing a good job. "You *lost* him?"

I don't even have the words for the dismay running through me. He may have been alive for a few years now, but he's still only kitten-size, something to do with the magic that made him. So many bad things could happen to my first kitten.

"It's okay, we'll find him. Everything was fine when I went to feed them this morning," Thomas assures me.

I take a deep breath. "So he's gone missing in the past few hours?" That's more of a relief than it should be.

"He's probably still in the flat," Daphne assures me.

I nod, remembering the last few times he'd escaped. I've found him all over the flat, normally in the kitchen where the food is.

"Erm, Mona," Ryan says.

"Yes?"

"I don't think Rhubarb's in the flat."

"Ryan!" Daphne scolds. "Are you trying to make this worse?"

He shakes his head and points to the

corner of the tent where my rucksack is squirming.

Oh no.

What has he done now?

"Mona?" Daphne says with hesitation in her voice. "What's going on?"

I sigh. "I think we've found Rhubarb."

I climb to my feet and make my way over to the bag, already knowing what I'm going to find.

Unless Ryan is wrong and it's a snake or scorpion, or anything else nasty that lives in the desert. But I doubt it. It's common practice to put a range of enchantments around dig sites, from those that make sure we have wifi, to ones that stop wildlife from entering, both to protect the people inside and the animals themselves.

I pull it open and sigh with relief.

"How did you manage that?" I ask the kitten as I scoop him up and take him back to the spot in front of the tablet. I hold him up so the others can see him.

"Phew. I guess we didn't lose him after all," Daphne says.

"And I'm guessing everything wasn't fine when you went to feed them," I tease.

"Sorry," Thomas mumbles.

"It's fine. They're all accounted for, even if this little rascal is up to mischief."

"He must have been protected by the enchantments on your bag," Ryan says.

"Which I must have cast too well," I mutter. Even with all the magic in the world, he still shouldn't have been able to get through all of the security checks we've been subjected to. Which only raises the question of how we're going to get him back home again. Can I hide him in my bag and stay calm while *knowing* he's there?

At least we have several weeks to figure it out.

"I'm glad he's okay," Caspian says.

"Me too." I scratch behind the fluffy grey ears.

Ryan glances at his watch. "It's nearly time for dinner," he warns me.

I nod. We don't want to be late for it, especially as this is our first day here. I'm not sure what time they'll stop serving and we don't want to be known as the interns who turn up and start demanding everything runs on our schedule. It's not a good look for anyone, especially when the career we want to be a part of is a small world where everyone knows everyone.

"We'll let you get to it," Daphne says. "We love you both."

"We love you too," I respond.

We wave goodbye and shut off the line.

I sigh. "One of these days you're going to get yourself into a lot of trouble," I tell my kitten.

"Meow?" he cocks his head to the side and gives me the huge eyes that always make me forgive him.

I sigh. "What am I going to do with you?"

"Take him everywhere you go so you don't have to worry about him causing more mischief?" Ryan quips.

I groan. "I thought we were past that."

"I don't think he's capable of not getting himself into trouble." He leans in and gives Rhubarb some friendly scratches before kissing my cheek.

"He's going to have to learn someday," I point out.

"And until then, I hope you have a pocket big enough to fit him in while we're having dinner."

"We can't take him with us..."

"Would you rather he gets bored of our tent and starts to go exploring and get himself into more trouble?"

I groan again. "Why is this happening?"

"Because you magically conjured a kitten who has the same cheeky streak as me."

"It's cute that the two of you think it's charming."

"Mona, it *is* charming. Otherwise you wouldn't love us as much." He hops to his feet, clearly ready to go and find out what the mess tent has to offer.

"I think you'll find I love you *despite* that," I mutter under my breath.

"Whatever the reason, it's far too late for you," he teases.

"Don't I know it."

Despite knowing it could end in disaster, I slip Rhubarb into one of the oversized pockets of my light jacket. At least the person who designed it didn't give it the same treatment as the rest of women's clothing gets and removed all the pockets.

"Behave," I instruct him.

"Meow."

"We both know you don't mean that."

He chuffs and burrows down to make himself comfortable.

If only he'd stay there.

Chapter 4

Excitement thrums through my entire being as we approach the dig site. I can't believe we're being given this opportunity. We may have had to jump through a lot of hoops to get it, and the likelihood of us witnessing a big discovery is slim, but I don't care. This is what I've dreamed of since I was a little girl, and the future I thought was taken from me when I discovered I was cursed. But now it's my reality. I'm here and I'll get to see a dig first hand. Nothing could be better.

Ryan slips a hand into mine and gives it a squeeze.

All right, so it *can* be better than just getting to witness a dig. I get to do it with someone I love by my side. A person who shares my fascinations even if our exact interests are slightly different.

Rhubarb squirms in my pocket, reminding me that we have a little hitchhiker along for the ride. He's been happy to stay hidden for now, but I'm not sure how long that's going to last. I know what Rhubarb is like and if I hadn't been so distracted by excitement, I would have checked my bag to make sure he didn't do anything like sneak along with us. But it's too late for regrets, especially when I'm secretly kind of glad he's here. It's nice to have a reminder of home who can't tease me.

"You could power a mansion off the nervous energy you're putting off," Ryan says, only going to prove my point.

"I can't help it. I'm excited."

"I know. Me too." He flashes me one of the most genuine smiles I think I've ever seen on him, reminding me that this isn't just my dream coming true, it's Ryan's too.

He's not here because I am. Even if he'd never met me, he'd want to be here. A warm surge of affection floods through me. I don't spend enough time considering what it means to share such an important part of my life with him, and I'm lucky I get to do this with him by my side.

"Maybe we'd have met at a dig site like this if we hadn't both gone to Grimalkin," he muses.

I chuckle. "Do you really think you'd be interested in me if I was covered in dust and sweating from the heat?"

He tugs me around and stops us both from walking.

"I'm not with you because you're beautiful," he reminds me. "Not that you aren't..." he scrambles to save himself.

I reach out and place a reassuring hand on his chest. "I know what you mean."

"Good. Because even when you have sand in your hair and sweat streaks on your face, there's nothing that can extinguish the light that shines from you. Especially when you're around something you're passionate about. *That's* why I love you. And why Caspian and Thomas do too. I think."

My lips curve up into a small smile. "You mean you don't sit around talking about all the reasons you love me with them?"

He shakes his head. "But maybe we should. Though perhaps we should save that for before a serious step in our relationship or I can see us having the conversation and instantly proposing to you or something."

My mouth falls open, but he doesn't elaborate on the statement. Instead, he pulls away and starts walking towards the dig site. It takes me a moment to realise I need to follow him if I don't want to be late and labelled a problem.

But I'll certainly be talking to Daphne about what he said later. She'll know the best way to respond. And she can suss out what my other two boyfriends think while they're taking care of my kittens. She has her own complicated love life, so she'll understand why I need to be certain about these things. I don't even know how they'd work, but having a best friend who will have to figure those things out at the same time is a relief.

But my romantic life isn't why I'm in Egypt and I need to focus if I'm going to make the most of this trip and impress enough people that I can get more experience next summer. And maybe some letters of recommendations. My chosen career path is going to be hard no matter what I do, though perhaps mine and Daphne's project on curse-breaking will help. *If* we can get the special commendation from the academy for it.

The two of us approach the table at the centre of the dig site. Sabine stands behind it wearing a similar getup to yesterday. Then again, that shouldn't be a surprise, I am too.

"Good. You're here. Both of you are going to be helping Vanessa with her excavation in the third sector." She points to a map of the site laid out in front of her.

I nod.

"She has all of the tools you need, do exactly what she says," Sabine instructs.

"Will do," I promise, meaning every word.

She dismisses us and we start to head in the direction the map indicated. I slip my hand into my pocket and give Rhubarb a quick scratch. He tries to catch my fingers with his paws to play, but I don't linger too long. If I do, it'll make the spell I put on my pocket to keep it cool enough for him useless. It's enough for me to know he's still there. I'll play with him when we get back to the tent to make up for it.

Everywhere I look there's something amazing. While a lot of it is still covered in sand, I can already make out the paintings and carvings on the temple walls. From the reports I've read of the dig, there hasn't been a translator sent yet, but it's only a matter of time.

To some extent, it doesn't matter what we're excavating. It's going to be an amazing discovery no matter what it is. Though I suppose it would be less exciting to learn we're uncovering an ancient toilet. But I don't think that's what this place is.

"You're doing it again," Ryan says.

"Doing what?"

"Bouncing with excitement."

"Aren't you?"

"Good point."

"I'm just excited to be here," I admit. "We're lucky that we managed to get the spots, they don't even always take interns at these kinds of digs." It's one of the things that makes getting an internship even more diffi-cult. They'll only take people who are quali-fied for the positions. Though a small part of me worries that they'll realise I'm not.

"I know," he assures me. "And we're going to make the most of it."

I don't think I've ever seen Ryan this serious about anything before. He's always the joker in the room, no matter who else is in it.

"Ah, interns," a woman I assume is Vanessa says, clapping her hands together in excitement. "Sabine told me you'd be joining me."

I smile at her. She seems nice, though I know appearances can be deceiving. "I'm Mona, this is Ryan."

"Good, good. Come with me and I'll set you off on your task," she instructs.

It strikes me that there seems to be a lot of travel involved in being on a dig, but I don't question it. Nothing about what's happening strikes me as odd.

She leads us to a covered part of the temple. The moment we step inside the difference in temperature hits me. It's much cooler in here where the sun hasn't reached. I'm glad to be able to do magic. Once we're settled in, I'll do a quick spell so I stay at the right temperature. Perhaps I should have done that before we left our tent, but I didn't think of it,

I was too focused on how to keep Rhubarb safe.

I check on him again. Something tells me I'm going to be doing that for the rest of the day.

"All right, this is where you're going to be working," Vanessa says, pointing to a sheet and tools laid out. "Sabine said you didn't have the right equipment yet?"

I shake my head. "We're still students."

"That's fair, I didn't get my first set of tools until after I graduated with my PhD. But if you get that far, you'll need them."

"I plan on getting that far," I assure her.

"We'll see. But for now, I've got you what you need from the store. They're not the best quality, but you'll be able to clean the sand away well enough."

It's grunt work at best, but I don't care. The chance to be around all of this is amazing enough.

"Oh, and no magic to do any of this. You can use it on yourselves if you're careful, but definitely no using it on any of the temple walls or artefacts. It can backfire too easily and potentially even trigger curses," she warns us.

We exchange a quick look.

"We'll be careful," Ryan promises.

Extra careful if I have anything to say about it. I've been cursed once in my life, I don't need it to happen a second time.

"Good. Then get to it." She walks off and leaves the two of us alone.

"I guess it's up to us to figure out what to do," Ryan mutters.

I frown. "Did you not read the information packet we were given?"

A sheepish look crosses his face. "No. I thought you would."

"I could be really mean and not tell you what you need to know."

"You wouldn't..."

"You're right." I lean in and kiss him on the cheek. "But you're reading it tonight."

He groans, but I know he will. He doesn't want to waste this opportunity any more than I do.

Chapter 5

I take a long drink of water. I don't think I can get enough of it in this heat. I certainly feel as if I'm sweating out just as much as I'm putting in. It's a good job Ryan met me before we started coming on digs after all. Then again, he fell in love with me while I was unable to do magic without producing a kitten and facing the prospect of failing out of the academy just because Mum's former best friend had a score to settle.

Rhubarb squirms in my pocket, then pops his head out to look around. A small part of me wants to tell him to get back in there so no one sees him, but the rest of me feels sorry for my kitten. I scoop him out and place him on the blanket between us.

I rip off a piece of bread and hold it out to him.

He cocks his head to the side and studies me.

"I'm sorry," I tell him. "But I don't have anything with me for you. That's what you get when you hitchhike."

Ryan chuckles. "You could use magic."

"That's not going to teach him a lesson," I point out even as I pull out my wand. Just because Rhubarb shouldn't be here, it doesn't mean that he should suffer.

I point my wand towards the bread and transform it into a piece of chicken with reasonable ease. It still surprises me when I manage to do magic without it backfiring, even if it's been years since the last kitten incident.

He takes the chicken between his paws and starts to eat, looking as adorable as normal in the process.

"Is it wise to have him out?" Ryan asks.

I shrug. "Technically there isn't anything in the dig rules about having pets here." Though

I suspect that's because it's common sense not to bring them.

"Maybe not. But this is Rhubarb. He makes me look sensible."

I snort. "He's a kitten."

"My point exactly. Mischief is his middle name."

"How can he have a middle name when he only has one to begin with?"

"Rhubarb Mischief Black. It has a nice ring to it, don't you think?"

I try to keep myself from laughing, but don't manage. "That's ridiculous."

"Mona..."

"He doesn't even have any official paperwork for me to use the name on."

"Mona," Ryan says again.

"Hmm?"

"He's gone."

My eyes widen as I take in the empty space between us where my kitten had been moments before.

I'm on my feet within seconds and scanning the surrounding area.

"He can't have gone far," Ryan assures me.

"Seriously? Weren't you just telling me

about how much trouble he can get into?" I try to keep the panic out of my voice. It won't help any of us, especially not the tiny kitten in a foreign environment with a lot of people who don't know about his existence.

"Mona, he's there. Look." Ryan points towards the entrance to the temple.

Sure enough, a small bundle of grey fur is skipping around between the stones. It's almost as if he's chasing something, but that doesn't seem likely with the charms that will be up around this place.

I don't hesitate and set off in the direction of the kitten with Ryan in tow behind me.

We hurry into the temple, turning at any sight of the mischievous kitten.

"Rhubarb?" I call. "Come back, it's not safe." I have no idea if pleading with him will work. or if warning him is even a good idea, but I have to try.

"There," Ryan says, pointing towards a thin crack in the temple wall.

I lurch forward to try and catch my kitten, hoping I'll manage. I can't resort to using magic while inside the temple without risking far more than alerting people to the fact my pet is here.

Rhubarb darts away from my hands and through the crack.

I close my eyes and take a deep breath.

Ryan places a comforting hand on my back. "It's fine, we'll get him back," he promises.

I fight back the tears threatening to fall. I should have sent him back home when we found him. Or sorted out some way to keep him in the tent, but that felt even crueler.

"Come on, it's big enough for us to slip through," Ryan says, already heading towards the crack. I want to tell him no, but it's too late, he's followed the kitten through.

I sigh and wipe my tears away. If I want to get out of this unscathed, then I have to pull myself together. The excavation has paused while the hottest parts of the day are passing, which means it'll be several hours before anyone notices we're not where we're supposed to be.

Hopefully, that's going to be enough time to find Rhubarb and figure out a way to stop him running off and causing trouble again.

Though if I'm honest, I've been trying to find that solution for years and have failed at every turn. At this rate, my entire life is going to be chasing after mischievous kittens.

With no other option presenting itself, I do the only thing I can think of and slip through the crack in the wall. While I don't think it's a proper doorway, it's easily big enough for me to get through.

I pass into a small tunnel and frown. This *does* make it seem like the crack is a door. Perhaps it's some kind of servants' passageway to help them appear and disappear without calling attention to themselves?

I push the thought aside and focus on the task at hand. I can see a small light up ahead, which I assume must be from Ryan's wand. The excavations haven't started in here, meaning there aren't any of the soft lights to guide my path. I pull out my wand and create one, making it float by the side of my head. If I've done the spell right, it should move with me, which should stop any accidental magic hitting the temple.

The walls on either side of me are begging for my attention with the beauty of the paintings. Even in a corridor like this that doesn't seem to have been a main one, they're intricate in a way we can't completely understand. There's a story on them that I can't wait to uncover.

But now isn't the time for it.

I hurry after Ryan and Rhubarb, hoping that nothing bad will happen to either of them.

Chapter 6

Nothing I do seems to stop the worries rushing through my head. There are so many things that could go wrong on a site like this. With no one having investigated this part of the site yet, there's the chance the structure isn't completely sound and could fall down around us. That's without taking freak sandstorms into account.

Or curses.

Or the fact that if anyone finds out about us being here, we could end up sent home on the first flight out tomorrow with no chance at all of being able to pursue the careers we want to.

I don't want any of that to happen.

A sigh of relief fills me as I turn a corner and find Ryan standing in front of me. At least one of them is safe. Now all we have to do is find Rhubarb and return through the twisting tunnels that brought us here. There seems to be a complicated warren of them, but we should be okay retracing our steps.

"Where is he?" I ask my boyfriend.

"Over there. But look." He points.

The reason he's standing so still becomes apparent to me as I follow his gaze.

My jaw drops at the sight in front of me. A huge statue of a cat-headed goddess domi-nates the room. She's magnificent in a way only these things can be.

And sitting on her knee is the object of my current frustration.

Rhubarb looks straight at me and licks his paw lazily, as if it's been his plan to bring me here all along. Perhaps it has, though that raises questions about how the kitten knew about the statue in the first place.

Ryan steps forward but I put out an arm to stop him.

"We have to check for curses," I warn him. While I'm hopeful there aren't any, we could cause a lot of damage if we make an assumption and are wrong.

"How are we going to do that? Neither of us have the training yet..."

I raise an eyebrow. "You really think Daphne and I haven't come up with a spell of our own to find curses?"

He sighs dramatically. "I should have known."

"Potentially yes. Most people do know their sister and girlfriend well enough to guess these things." I pull out my wand.

"Is it really a good idea to cast an untested spell though?" he asks.

"Who says it's untested?"

"You cursed yourself again to do it, didn't you?"

I shake my head. "We cursed an apple."

"I hope you didn't leave it lying around after."

"We ate it."

"Mona..."

"Don't worry, we took the curse off first, we're not idiots," I assure him.

"All right, but if this goes wrong..."

"You'll share the blame with me because that's the you thing to do," I finish.

"It's scary how well you know me sometimes."

I step away from him to give myself space and take a deep breath. He's not wrong about the spell I'm about to use being relatively untested. But I have to trust in the research Daphne and I have done. We put a lot of work into it so we can be sure that our project gets the right consideration next year. We want to be on the honour roll for it.

I close my eyes and wave my wand, thinking of the spell we created. Technically, there are some words for it if I want to use them, but I always feel silly saying them out loud, and as it's a spell of my co-creation, I don't think I need them to direct it properly.

A thin sheet of blue stretches out over everything in front of me, shimmering as it touches the different parts of the room.

"Wow," Ryan mutters.

"Right?" I can't help the pride that wells up within me as I watch the spell settle.

"What does it all mean?" he asks.

"There's curse residue on a few of the

objects." I point them out among the treasures piled at the goddess' feet. "But there aren't any active curses."

I don't wait for him to respond to stride forward. The goddess is much bigger than me, with her knee coming up to most of my height. I scoop my errant kitten from her.

"Don't do that to me again," I whisper to him, my voice cracking as I do. I can't imagine losing him. He means too much to me.

I clutch the kitten to my chest, where he nestles as if asking for my forgiveness. My heart warms as the relief sets in.

"I'm going to put you back in my pocket now," I tell him. "You have to stay there."

"Meow."

It might just be me, but I think he sounds almost as if he regrets running away.

"Problem solved?" Ryan asks.

"Yes. But we should take a photo of this to show Sabine."

"Are you sure? Then we'll have to explain what we were doing here."

"And if she finds out we *didn't* tell her about the kind of find that could make her career?" I point out. "She'll get the credit for this and be set for life. I have to imagine that will outweigh the fact we're out of bounds." Though technically, we haven't been told where we can and can't go.

He sighs. "You're the boss."

"No, I'm not. We're in this together. If you want to stay quiet then we can," I promise, meaning every word. I don't think it's the best course of action, but I don't want Ryan to have to do something he's uncomfortable with. That would make me a terrible girlfriend.

"I think you're right," he says. "We should tell her and hope she doesn't send us home. Maybe she'll even be grateful enough to give us some of the credit?" It's hard to miss the hopeful note in his voice.

I get it. There's a little part of me that wonders the same. But regardless of whether she'll let us share in the glory of the find, we need to tell her about it. There's so much that could be learned from the treasure trove around us.

I pull out my phone and bring up the camera. The curse finding spell seems to have worn off enough that it doesn't show on it, which is good. While going out of bounds is probably forgivable, I don't think using magic would be, even if it hasn't done any harm.

We both set about taking as many photos as possible, with Rhubarb watching intently from my pocket but not making any moves to try and escape again. Maybe he was trying to bring us to this place after all.

My gaze flickers up to the cat-headed goddess. I'm not sure whether I believe in the existence of any gods, old or new, but considering magic is in my blood, I'm not sure I can totally discount their existence.

"Mona," Ryan says, a hint of worry in his voice.

"Hmm?"

"You've got to come see this."

I wonder what he's found? I drop my phone back into my pocket and make my way over to the other side of the statue where Ryan is taking his.

It only takes me a moment to work out what he wants me to see. A silver teapot sits among the treasure.

"That doesn't fit the time period," Ryan whispers.

"Not in the slightest. The design doesn't match the location either."

"Did they even have teapots back then?"

I shake my head. "I think the first teapot was made in the fifteen hundreds some time."

"How do you even know that?"

The blood rushes to my cheeks. "I like to look up random facts so Daphne will let me be on her pub quiz team."

"She lets you do that?"

"Only because I was able to answer a question about who invented the sandwich one time."

He cocks his head to the side. "Who did?"

"The Earl of Sandwich," I mutter.

"Seriously? It's named after an Earl?"

I shrug. "He didn't want to get his fingers dirty while gambling."

"That actually makes sense..."

"But it doesn't solve the mystery of the teapot," I point out.

"Do we have to solve it? Can't we just let Sabine figure it out?"

"I guess so? The style looks to be Moroccan, but there isn't anything else here that looks to have the same origin."

"Then let's not worry about it. Smarter people than us can work it out."

The curiosity is going to eat away at me until someone does, but he's right. We should focus on the rest of what's here.

We take photos of the rest of it and then start to head back. I don't know how much time has passed, but now that we're going to tell people where we've been, I guess it's not as important that no one notices we're gone.

But now I have another reason to want to get back. I'm excited to tell Sabine about what we've discovered and to uncover more about it.

Chapter 7

I scratch the top of Rhubarb's head as we walk back in the direction we came. Something about the wall paintings feels off, though, and I can't put my finger on what. I don't remember feeling this ominous about them on the way in.

"What's wrong?" Ryan asks.

"How do you know something's wrong?" A small quiver comes through my voice, making the answer clear.

"I can tell."

I sigh. "I don't know. Something feels off, but I can't work out what."

"Do you think it was the treasure? Was it cursed after all?"

I shake my head. "My spell wouldn't fail."

Even so, I stop him from working and pull out my wand. With a wave, I cast the same curse finding spell over the three of us.

The thin blue shimmer settles over us, only to dissipate within an instant.

"Nothing."

Ryan stares at me with adoration in his eyes.

"What?"

"You're amazing, did you know that?"

I glance away, unable to take the intensity.

"I mean it, Mona. Most people would shy away from curses after what you went through. And away from creating their own spells in case they backfire. But you've just used it to become even more of the person you want to be. It's amazing."

"Thank you," I mutter.

He steps forward and wraps an arm around me, pulling me closer to him.

"I mean it."

"I know you do," I admit.

"And I love you."

"I love you too."

This might not be the place for it, but I

don't think that matters. My eyes flutter closed as his lips meet mine and he kisses me with all the tenderness of years of a relationship. He knows just how to make me feel admired and cherished, even if he is the joker. Maybe that's what makes it so I feel this way. When he's serious, he really means what he's saying, and I'm honoured to be able to see that side of him.

The ground around us shakes, but it isn't until Ryan pulls away from me that I realise it's not in my head.

"What was that?" he asks.

"An earthquake?" I whisper.

"It's got to be."

"Do you think it's over or is there going to be more to come?" I try not to let my nerves come through my voice.

Rhubarb buries himself in my pocket, either sensing my distress, or not liking the way the earthquake felt.

"I don't know. But we should get out of here in case it does," he suggests.

I nod eagerly, not particularly wanting to get trapped in a temple when no one knows where we are. We can probably still call someone for help, but I'd prefer not to if we don't have to. Things are going to go much smoother if we can broach the topic of what we've found in our own way rather than seeming like we're covering our tracks because we caused problems.

"Come on." I take his hand and pull him along with me so that we can get back to the crack in the wall that we came in through. As far as I can tell we're going the right way, but I'm not completely sure about that.

I wonder if I should set Rhubarb down so he can lead us out of here. It's his fault that we're in this predicament in the first place. But that's just giving in to my fear. It's going to be fine. The earthquake was only quick, there's a good chance that nothing has been dislodged and we're going to be fine. This place has been standing for thousands of years, there's no telling how many earthquakes it's withstood in its time as a result. I just need to trust the long-dead builders did their job properly.

I don't relax until the corridor becomes more familiar and looks like the one we came through at the start of this. There's even light coming through the crack in the wall.

"See, we're fine, nothing bad has happened," Ryan assures me.

"Why would you say that before we're out of here?" The fact he wants to jinx this is mildly amusing to me.

"Sorry, I'll keep quiet." He draws his hand across his lips to pretend to zip them.

I suppress a laugh, enjoying the relief of being close to the exit.

I step forward, only to be stopped in my tracks when another tremor starts to take over. Something tells me this one is going to be worse than the previous one.

"Get down," I half-shout to Ryan, despite the fact he's right next to me.

I turn in time to see a large piece of rock hurtle towards him. I let out a shriek even as I grab the wand from my pocket.

But I'm too slow. The rock strikes Ryan on the head and his face goes instantly blank.

Shock travels through me until I realise that I can't let it beat me or we're going to be in more trouble.

I coax Rhubarb out of my pocket so I can shelter him properly. I curl up in a ball on the floor even as sand starts to rain down on me.

With a quick flick of my wand I create a shield around the three of us. I need to check on Ryan, but I can't until it's safe for me to move around more. While I'm reasonably certain my shield will hold, it's been made in haste which is always the way that mistakes happen, especially when there's rubble falling down around us.

I breathe deeply, trying to keep myself calm. Rhubarb presses up against my arm where I'm sheltering him.

"It's okay," I promise him, hoping I'm not lying. "We're going to be okay."

If I repeat it to myself enough, then perhaps I'll start believing it. Maybe.

I reach out to touch Ryan's prone form. His chest is still moving as he breathes, which is a relief. Once I'm sure there aren't any more shockwaves, I'll do a proper check of him, but for now, that's enough.

Chapter 8

Ryan groans and his eyes flutter open, sending relief crashing through me.

"Ryan?" I whisper.

"What happened?" he croaks.

"You got hit on the head."

"Oh, right. Earthquake."

"Ah, so you remember. That's good." I scratch Rhubarb behind the ears.

"Yes. I just have a bit of a headache."

"Not a surprise. I couldn't find any other injuries, but you're going to need to get checked out properly once we're out of here."

"I promise. But how likely is that going to be?" he asks.

"I haven't checked it out yet. I haven't left

your side. I didn't want you to wake up and think something bad had happened."

"You mean worse than a cave in when no one knows where we are?"

"Yes, that. At least we probably don't have to worry about getting bitten by anything nasty."

"Unless Rhubarb has fleas," he mutters.

"He does *not* have fleas." I hug my kitten tightly. "I do spells to make sure none of them do. They're healthy kittens."

"I know, I'm just teasing."

I give him a tight smile. "Let's get out of here before we do that."

I finally let the shield around us fall and get to my feet. There's still a danger of us ending up being squashed if there are more stones to fall, but I think we're mostly past that now.

"Dare I ask about the accessibility of the door?" he asks hesitantly.

"It's completely blocked." I gesture in the direction we originally came from, trying not to let the panic about what's happened overtake me.

"Ah. That's a problem."

"Just a small one."

"We can sort it out," he promises.

"We're going to have to or else the bodies the team are going to find are ours," I mutter.

"At least Sabine is a necromancer."

I startle. "She is?" I assumed she was a witch.

"Just a theory based on circumstantial evidence. But almost everyone is in agreement that she's one of the foremost experts on mummies, right?"

"That doesn't mean she's a necromancer."

"Maybe I'm wrong. But I don't think so."

"It hardly matters anyway. They can't raise the dead."

"We don't know that..."

"I'm not taking my chances that if we die, someone *may* be able to resurrect us. I'm going to go with trying to get out of here, still very much alive." I fix him a stern look so he realises that's the *only* option. There's no way I'm going to end up dying here. And neither is he. The three of us are going to get out of here and then we'll lead everyone to the treasure and all will be forgiven.

I get to my feet and make my way over to

the pile of rubble in front of the crack in the wall. It appears as if everything has just fallen straight in front of it and not that the door itself has collapsed. That's a start. It still poses a few problems, including that we're not supposed to use magic on the walls in the temple.

But there's no other way of getting out of here that won't take weeks. And I'm already starting to suffer from the lack of water. I guess I could try and change some of the stones into food and water, but that's not necessarily going to work. It's much easier to change stuff that's already edible into food. And that kind of negates the not using magic on the temple rule.

Ryan groans as he stands up, probably aching from the fall. He makes his way over to join me as I place Rhubarb carefully back into my pocket. He burrows down and makes himself comfortable, no longer the same mischievous kitten that got us into this mess. At least he's not making this any harder than it has to be.

"Do you want to hold the roof up while I

move the bricks?" Ryan asks. "I'd offer to do the holding, but..."

"If you have a concussion it's better that you don't do the bit that could kill us if it goes wrong," I finish for him.

"It's not a bad plan, but we need to make sure we're not going to set off any traps or anything..."

"You mean beyond making an earthquake?"

I snort. "Even you aren't that good a kisser."

"Hmm I need to try harder to shatter your world then," he quips.

"Only once we're out of here."

"Fine by me. I have you all to myself for the next few weeks and our tent is just out there."

"If we're not kicked off the dig."

"We won't be after we tell them about the treasure. It's going to be fine, Mona, I promise." He reaches out and touches a gentle hand to my back, giving me the reassurance he knows that I need.

I sigh. "I hope you're right."

"Will your curse detector spell work to find

traps?"

I shrug. "Only one way to find out." I flick my wand and send the spell out towards the rubble. It shimmers and flickers.

One patch flashes gold, then fades away.

"What does that mean?" There's a hint of fear in Ryan's voice. Perhaps he's taking things a little more seriously than I think he is.

"That's an old curse." Or it should be. Daphne and I haven't done as much testing of the spell as we'd like. Mostly because we don't have a lot of previously cursed items hanging around. Unless we count me.

"Old as in..."

"Won't hurt us, yes."

"Are you sure?"

Instead of answering, I point my wand at myself and cast the same spell, knowing what will happen when I do. The same gold hue glitters against my skin, except for the pocket where Rhubarb is that remains blue.

"Interesting," he says.

"Okay, so we're good with getting out of here?"

"If you think it's safe."

"Only one way to find out." But I'll make

sure to cast the spell strong enough against the roof to make sure we're protected. I don't think it'll be completely foolproof, but it's better to try than not.

"Ready when you are," Ryan says.

I touch my pocket to make sure Rhubarb is still curled up and safe, and am reassured by the warm ball inside it. I don't think he's going to be causing many problems for us from now on.

I pull my magic from deep within me and cast a spell that should help to hold the roof up. It should last long enough for Ryan to do his thing.

"Your turn."

He nods and turns his attention to the pile of rubble between us and our freedom. He mutters under his breath, probably choosing to use words to direct his spell just in case he has a concussion.

The grating sound of stone against stone fills the air, but I grit my teeth and put up with it. If it means we'll be able to get out of here, then it's worth a bit of auditory discomfort.

It takes Ryan a few goes to get enough of the stones moved away to the side.

Light comes streaming in from the crack in the wall. It's faint at first, but grows with strength as more of the exit is revealed to us.

We're going to get out of this unscathed. Somehow.

Maybe I need to start believing in the old gods after all. It almost feels as if we've been protected.

"All right, I think I'm done," Ryan says.

I grimace at the exhaustion written all over his face. Once we've talked to Sabine, I'm going to have to order him to the medical tent and then rest.

"I'll keep my spell up until we're outside." I don't think the roof is going to collapse, but I'm not going to risk it.

A grin spreads over his face. "We've done it, Mona," he says.

I smile back at him. "For now. We need to try and not lose our jobs too," I remind him.

"I think we'll be fine."

Not for the first time, I find myself envying Ryan's confidence. But that's okay. He's been helping me get through things with it for years, which is good enough for me.

I hold out my hand and he takes it.

The two of us make our way out of the temple and towards the main camp where we have to admit to what we've done. Even if the damage to the site wasn't our fault, I still feel as if it is. I just hope Sabine has it in her heart to forgive us.

Chapter 9

"Let me get this straight, the two of you went into the temple unsupervised and then went in even further to parts that haven't been checked for safety yet?" Sabine demands, looking between the two of us as if we're crazy.

In her defence, there's a good chance we are. When she puts it the way she just has, it doesn't sound good.

"Yes," Ryan says.

"Why would you do something so reckless?" She almost sounds more exasperated than angry, which is probably a good sign for us.

We exchange a glance. The only way we're not going to end up in a lot of trouble is if we tell the truth. And even then, it might backfire on us.

"My kitten escaped and ran into the temple, we were trying to get him back," I admit.

She raises an eyebrow. "Your kitten? Why would you bring a kitten on a dig?"

"I didn't," I admit sheepishly. "I didn't know he was here until it was too late."

"Are you trying to tell me you were outsmarted by a kitten?" Sabine asks.

"A magical kitten," Ryan interjects. "Mona made him."

I blush.

"That's very advanced magic," Sabine says.

"It was a curse," I admit. "In my first year at Grimalkin, I ended up with a curse that produced kittens every time I did magic."

"You have more than one?"

"Eleven." It sounds crazy now I'm saying it out loud, but there's nothing else I can say about it when it's the truth.

"Eleven kittens?"

I nod.

"And I'm assuming this is why you're the best curse-breaker in your class?"

"Is that what Thomas, sorry Mr Smith, told you?" Ryan asks.

"No. That's what one of the recommendations from Mona's professors said. It went on to say that if I thought there were any curses on the site, that I should ask an *intern* about how to spot them early."

"She and my sister created a spell for that," Ryan says eagerly.

I close my eyes and try not to get too embarrassed. I know he's only telling her these things because he's proud of me, but it makes it sound as if I think I'm better than people who have been doing this for years.

"Interesting," Sabine says. "And where is your sister? I only saw one application for a Chambers."

"She's back at the academy. She's still trying to work out what she wants to be. Personally, I think she'll end up in politics of some kind."

I raise an eyebrow. He's never told me that. I can see Daphne going that way one day, but maybe not yet.

"But she enjoys making up spells?" Sabine asks.

"Daphne likes to do anything that challenges her," I supply. "Hence the spells."

"Ah. I see. Well, I'd be interested to see this curse detecting spell before I decide what to do with the two of you."

"We found something while we were in the temple," I blurt. That's not how I intended to tell her, but I guess it will do.

"Oh?"

I pull out my phone and open the photo gallery to show her. I hand it over, hating to let someone else take possession of my phone, but knowing this could make all the difference when it comes to whether or not she'll let the two of us stay on the dig or not.

Sabine flicks through the photos, her eyes wide with amazement. I'm not surprised. I still feel that way about what we saw too.

"How did you find this?" she whispers.

"Rhubarb took us to it."

"Rhubarb?"

As if responding to his name, the tiny kitten pops his head out of my pocket and looks around.

"Meow."

"Ah. I see. He took you to the statue?"

I nod. "Ryan has more photos too."

"Including an odd teapot," he says. "It was out of place."

"A teapot? That would be an amazing find, it would completely change the way we see the ancient world..."

"It's not the right fit for the temple," I say quickly. "It appears to be Moroccan in origin, and it looks far newer. There wasn't anything else I noticed that matched it in style or age."

"Hmm. That's odd."

Very. The more I think about the teapot, the more confused I am about its presence. Why is something from medieval Morocco at the earliest among treasures from Ancient Egypt?

"I'll set a team on clearing the path today. I think it's best if Ryan gets checked out by a medic and rests up before we excavate the chamber the two of you found."

"We?" I whisper.

"I'm assuming you want to be part of the team that does that to learn about what you discovered."

I exchange a quick glance with Ryan.

"We just assumed you wouldn't want us there," I admit softly.

"Ah, I see. I'm not in the habit of taking credit from the people who deserve it, especially when I get part of it anyway as it's my dig. The two of you will be there and will get the credit you deserve once the authenticity of the find is confirmed. Which I assume it will, I doubt two students could pull off a scam like this."

"We would never." I can't keep the shock out of my voice.

"Besides, if you're as good of a curse-breaker as your professor says, then I suspect our paths will be crossing on multiple occasions in the years to come. In a profession as small as ours, I find it's best not to step on toes unless you can't avoid it. Even if those toes belong to an intern at the time," Sabine says.

"Oh." I can't think of more of a response than that. My mind is still reeling from the fact she thinks I have a potential career in the field I want to work in. I know it's tough to get a start in archaeology. That's one of the reasons I'm here.

"Thank you," Ryan says.

Ah, that would have been a good choice.

"Now get medical attention, food, and rest. You both have the rest of the day off, but I expect you to report first thing tomorrow," she instructs, handing me back my phone.

I nod, still unable to speak.

Sabine flashes the two of us a genuine smile as she passes and heads towards one of the teams heading up excavations.

It isn't until she's gone that I let out an excited laugh.

"We've done it," I whisper.

"Made the impression we wanted to? You're damn right we have," Ryan responds.

"I'm glad you're here with me."

"Me too." He starts to sway back and forth. I reach out and steady him.

"All right, time to get to the medic."

"But we need to tell Daph and the others about this," he protests.

I chuckle. "We'll do that once we're back at the tent," I promise, looking forward to the conversation more than ever. They all know why we came here and I can't wait to tell them that it worked.

Chapter 10

The knock sounds while I'm still wrapped in a towel and nowhere near ready, which can only mean it must be Daphne. She's either forgotten I have a date tonight, or something urgent needs my attention.

"Come in," I call, grabbing an oversized t-shirt from nearby and pulling it over my head. I don't mind my best friend seeing me in nothing more than a towel, but it's always better to have something on.

The door cracks open, which is a beacon for Felix, who rushes towards it, hellbent on managing to escape.

"Whoa, that's not for you," Caspian says,

scooping the kitten up. "You're getting bold in your old age."

I let out a squeak. He's not supposed to be here yet.

"I'm sorry, I'm not ready yet..."

"I know. I'm early."

I narrow my eyes, trying to work out what he has planned. Which is hard when he hasn't told me anything about the date we're supposed to be going on.

A sheepish expression crosses his face. "I thought you might have missed the kittens while you were away."

"Except for Rhubarb," I mutter. I still don't know how the little rascal managed to creep into my bags without me or Ryan noticing *and* get to a completely different country without customs noticing. If this kind of behaviour continues then I'm going to have to register him for a pet passport.

Caspian chuckles. "He's still in the bad books?"

"All is forgiven. He did help us make a discovery no one else our age could have ever found," I point out.

"True. But anyway, I thought you might want to spend some time with them tonight."

"But it's our date..."

"That's what this is for." He lifts the hand holding the bag. "I have everything we need for a fun night in. Your favourite snacks, a movie you've seen so many times you don't need to pay proper attention to so we can set it up, and one of my hoodies that hasn't been in the wash yet."

I chuckle. "That was a downside of going on a dig somewhere hot, I couldn't take one with me."

"Next time you should go to the Arctic for one."

"I don't think they do much archaeology up there."

"Then you can be the one who starts it. I can imagine the headlines now. *Monica Black makes yet another discovery...*"

An amused smile spreads over my face. "Why don't I go get some drinks and you can set up my room just how you want it?"

"I have drinks, we just need glasses." He frowns. "And maybe plates. I brought cake and I know you don't like crumbs in the bed."

I shake my head in amusement but lean up to kiss his cheek as I pass anyway. As much fun as I had on the dig with Ryan, I missed them all terribly. One of the good things about academy living is that we're all so close together, but it makes for a lonely time when I'm away from two of my boyfriends, my best friend, and most of my kittens.

A warm fuzzy feeling settles within me at the thought of what Caspian is doing for me by letting us have the date in my room. He isn't wrong, I have missed the kittens and their mischief. At some point in the past few years, I've become a crazy kitten lady through and through. Though I may have three too many romantic partners for the stereotype to truly hold up.

"What are you doing here? I thought you had a date?" Daphne asks as I enter the kitchen.

"I do, Caspian brought movie night to me."

"Ah, that's sweet."

"It is." I sigh wistfully.

"Thanks for not killing my brother while you were away," my best friend teases.

I snort. "You realise I love him, right?"

"So do I. Though admittedly not in the same way. I think that's part of the reason I *do* want to kill him sometimes."

"Oh, Daph."

She laughs.

"He wasn't the main problem."

"Ah, right. Rhubarb."

"We should have known." I reach up into the cupboard and pull out two glasses and two plates to take back to my room.

"Maybe in another three years we'll be certain of what that little kitten can accomplish."

"By which point he'll already have taken over the world," I quip.

"Most likely. I can see it in his eyes."

I chuckle at the mental image of Rhubarb sitting on a throne and lording it over us all. He's definitely capable of it.

"Have fun on your date," Daphne says as I wave goodbye to her. "Don't do anything I wouldn't do."

Not for the first time, I'm glad it's not her brother waiting for me. Thankfully, we've managed to keep embarrassing sibling confusion to a minimum, though I never thought dating my best friend's brother would be *this* complicated.

I lean back against my bedroom door to push inside. Caspian has created what looks almost like a blanket fort in my absence. He must have used magic, there's no way he could have pulled this off in such a short time frame otherwise.

"Aren't we a little old for setups like this?" I ask while secretly hoping he'll say no.

"Never." He takes the plates and glasses from me and places them inside the fort.

"Do you want me to change?" I gesture down to the long t-shirt. I'm not sure if it's his, or one of the others.

He shakes his head. "I brought sweatpants so we could match."

"That's why you turned up early, isn't it?" I take a seat inside the fort and lean back against the mountain of cushions he's pulled out from under my bed. I started keeping some there once it became clear we all couldn't hang out in my room without some- where to sit and whoever designed the dorm rooms didn't think about what people would need if they have multiple partners.

"You bet. I didn't want you to get all dressed up when comfort is the aim of the night." He blows me a kiss and heads off to the bathroom to change. I'm not sure why he bothers, it's nothing I haven't seen before.

Isla climbs onto my knee and curls up in a ball. I stroke her absentmindedly, enjoying the comforting feeling of a kitten there. I missed them more than I thought I would while I was away. Though that's something I'm going to have to get used to if I want to follow the career path I have in mind. Either that, or I find a way to take them with me.

I'm not sure how practical that is, though.

Caspian returns and sits himself down next to me, holding his arm out. I snuggle into him, loving that he's thought to do this. I love going on fun dates, but I'm not with any of them so they'll take me to fancy places. The moments I can spend with them like this are even better than that. It's true to the people we are and who we want to be.

It makes me believe that I can build a life that includes everything I want it to.

I sigh and rest my head on Caspian's shoulder. He squeezes me tightly and kisses the top of my head softly.

I close my eyes, enjoying the closeness. I never imagined things could be this perfect. Not with him, not with the others, and certainly not with the eleven mischievous kittens who are playing around us.

Whatever I did to deserve this, I'm grateful. There's nothing I want to change about the life we have. I know there will still be challenges in our future, but with them by my side, I know we can conquer anything.

Epilogue

I smooth down the sparkling black dress that makes me feel as if I'm at a movie premiere. Except that I'm not. This is *so* much better than that.

Thomas holds out his arm to me and I slip my own through to rest my hand on his. Just like the other two, he's looking rather dashing in a formal tuxedo.

"Are you ready for this?" he asks.

I let out a nervous laugh. "Yes and no."

"I think you're one of the youngest people to ever be honoured by the museum."

"Is that supposed to make me feel better?" I raise an eyebrow.

"Sorry, I didn't mean to..."

"It's fine, Thomas, don't worry. I just wish Rhubarb could be here to get the honour too. Without him, we'd never have found the treasure." I sigh, thinking of my kittens back in my dorm room. I missed them all dearly on the dig. I'm definitely going to have to work out a way to take them with me in the future or I'm going to end up hating my job.

Daphne is ahead of us, dragging Ryan from exhibit to exhibit as we make our way to the main party.

"Do you have a second spare arm?" Caspian asks as he appears to my side.

"I do." I thread it through his so I have one of them on each side. Luckily, I don't have a bag to get in the way after I stashed my phone in Caspian's pocket earlier on.

No one pays any attention to us as we enter the main room the museum is using for the party. If Sabine is to be believed, this is one of the last times I can expect that to be true. She seems to have decided that she's going to help me realise my dream of becoming an archaeological curse-breaker. Not that I'm complaining. She's renowned for what she does and it's a great opportunity for me.

"Ah, there you are, Mona. Thomas, nice to see you again," the woman in question says as she strides towards us with a wide smile on her face.

She looks so different from while we were on the dig site, though I suspect the same is true of me. Her dark hair is loose and styled into slick waves and her sleeveless dress shows off a sleeve of tattoos I didn't know she had.

"And this must be the other boyfriend," she says.

Thomas shoots me a confused look.

"Yes, this is Caspian."

He holds out his hand. "It's a pleasure to meet you, I've heard a lot about you."

"I should hope so," Sabine responds while taking him up on his handshake. "Where is Ryan?" she asks me.

"I think he's showing Daphne some of the exhibits," I respond.

"More like Daphne is showing him," Thomas mutters.

I snort. "Sorry. Look for the witch with bright pink hair, you can't miss her." That's certainly one advantage of Daphne's styling choice.

Sabine nods. "I'm looking forward to meeting her. But don't go too far, you'll be needed soon."

I give her a weak smile, suddenly starting to get nervous about all the people here knowing what I'm capable of.

She waves and heads off in the twins' direction.

"Why don't you show us the treasure?" Thomas asks.

I nod and lead them over to the display. The huge case is filled with jewel-like colours and glittering gold. In some ways, it's even more beautiful here than it was in the pile at Bastet's feet. A small part of me is sad about it being taken away from its rightful home. But the collection is only on loan to the museum. It will be heading back to Egypt after a brief stint here. It feels right to do that. It belongs to the country it was found in.

"They're amazing," Caspian says as he studies them. "I'm so proud of you, Mona."

"We all are," Thomas puts in.

"It wouldn't have happened if you hadn't put in a good word for us," I remind him.

Thomas shrugs. "We're a team. You know that. This time, you and Ryan have succeeded for us. Before long it'll be me or Caspian."

"You say that as if you haven't already been published in a journal," I remind him.

"I don't think that's quite the same as finding one of the biggest hauls of treasure in the past decade."

"How am I even going to live up to that?" I ask, despair in my voice.

"You will," Caspian assures me. "You have amazing things ahead of you."

I hope he's right. I don't want this to be the best I ever achieve. But with Sabine as a mentor, I don't think that's going to be the case. By the time I graduate with my doctorate in a few years, I'll have had the opportunity to work on several digs with her. And maybe if I prove my worth, I'll even be able to get paid for some extra curse-breaking too.

I can hope.

I do another walk up and down the case, looking at each artefact in turn.

"That's odd," I whisper.

"What is?" Caspian asks.

"Remember the teapot I told you about?"

He nods.

"It's not here."

"Maybe they decided not to display it," Thomas suggests. "Sometimes they do that."

"Hmm. Maybe. It doesn't fit with the rest of it." I push the thought out of my mind. It doesn't really matter where it's gone, that doesn't diminish the discovery we've made in any way.

"Mona, I think they're ready for you," Caspian says, pointing to where Sabine is waving me over.

I plaster a smile on my face and make my way to her. Everything starts to pass in a haze. I'm not sure I can deal with all the eyes looking at me as Sabine makes her way up to the stand to make a speech.

She goes through the normal pleasantries of thanking the museum and the financial backers of the dig, along with everyone who played a role in it.

"...and I'd like to give a special thanks to the two budding young archaeologists who were instrumental in the discovery of the artefacts on display here, Monica Black and Ryan Chambers." She gestures to us as applause sounds from around the room.

Ryan's hand finds mine and gives it a squeeze as we both smile and wave at the crowd.

I'm still in a little disbelief that this is happening. I'm getting everything I've ever wanted for a start to a career and more. I haven't even graduated yet, though that's coming up soon, and the chances are looking good that Daphne and I will get on the honour roll like we want.

It's hard to believe that nearly four years ago I had no real friends, no love life, and a curse that stopped me from using the magic I'd been able to do my entire life. Especially when I now have a best friend who is like a sister to me, three adoring boyfriends, enough kittens to last a lifetime, and a promising future career.

It seems that everything has worked out just fine in the end.

Thank you for reading *This Time Is Trouble*, I hope you enjoyed it! If you want to know more about the whereabouts of the teapot Mona and Ryan found, more will be revealed in the *Cauldron Coffee Shop* Series, starting with *Pumpkin Spice And All Things Nice*: https://books.authorlauragreenwood.co.uk/pumpkinspiceandallthingsnice

Or, if you want to read more about Grimalkin Academy, you can start Daphne's story in *Catching A Vampire*: https://books.authorlauragreenwood.co.uk/catchingavampire

Author Note

Thank you for reading *This Time Is Trouble*, I hope you enjoyed Mona's happy ever after story - especially as she gets to live out her dream unencumbered by her curse (even if she does have to leave two of her boyfriends, and most of her kittens, back at the academy while she's on her internship - but don't worry, they were waiting for her to get back!)

While I've known what Mona (and the guys) were going to do after they finished at Grimalkin Academy for a while, *This Time Is Trouble* wasn't actually planned to be a story until much later when the characters for an upcoming series of mine, *Cauldron Coffee Shop* started talking to me. The leader of the dig, Sabine, is the character who links the two series when she sends some treasure to her best friend/coffee shop owner, Willow.

Cauldron Coffee Shop follows witch, Willow, as she goes through the day-to-day life of a magical coffee shop owner...if day-to-day life includes finding an ancient cursed warlock hiding in a teapot!

If you prefer the academy setting, then Grimalkin Academy will be the setting for a series coming next year, but until then, there are two new academies in the same world that have series coming this year - *Sabre Woods Academy* is where big cat shifters in *The Obscure World* go, and *Scythe Grove Academy* is for the reapers.

And finally, if you liked the slight Egyptian theme of *This Time Is Trouble*, then I have plenty of series for you to try! If you've read a lot of my books, you may already have picked up on how much I love Egyptology, and study it a lot for the fun of it. If you want more, you can try my *Forgotten Gods* or *The Apprentice Of Anubis* series.

If you want to keep up to date with new releases and other news, you can join my Facebook Reader Group or mailing list.

Stay safe & happy reading!

- Laura

Download a Free
Grimalkin Academy Story

All curses start somewhere, and it's not always where you expect.

With graduation approaching, Ronnie and Magda need to finish writing their spellbook so they can receive the ultimate reward: a place on Grimalkin Academy's honour roll.

But when things start to go wrong, it turns out that more than their friendship is on the line, and if Ronnie can't fix it, the consequences won't be worth thinking about.

-

Curses Start Somewhere is a prequel to Grimalkin Academy, an urban fantasy academy series featuring two best friends, lots of kittens, and a low-heat poly romantic subplot.

If you enjoy paranormal academy, cute familiars, light-hearted romance, witches, and friendship, you should start the Grimalkin Academy series today.

You can download your copy of Curses Start Somewhere here: https://books.authorlauragreenwood.co.uk/ronnieandmagda

Also by Laura Greenwood

You can find out more about each of my series on my website.

- The Apprentice Of Anubis: an urban fantasy series set in an alternative world where the Ancient Egyptian Empire never fell. It follows a new apprentice to the temple of Anubis as she learns about her new role.
- Forgotten Gods: a paranormal adventure romance series inspired by Egyptian mythology. Each book follows a different Ancient Egyptian goddess.
- Jinx Paranormal Dating Agency: a paranormal romance series based on worldwide mythology where paranormals and deities take part in events organised by the Jinx Dating Agency. Each book follows a different couple.
- House Of Blood And Roses: a vampire romantasy series following a heroine who discovers she's a vampire noble

and has to navigate a world full of politics, betrayal, and blood lust.

- Amethyst's Wand Shop Mysteries (with Arizona Tape): an urban fantasy murder mystery series following a witch who teams up with a detective to solve murders. Each book includes a different murder.
- Scales Of Justice: an urban fantasy following a thief who accidentally becomes the newest apprentice of the goddess of truth.
- Purple Oak Oasis (with Ariana Jade): a cozy fantasy romance series with unusual magic. Each book follows a different couple.
- Falhaven Castle: a cozy fantasy romance series following a princess who just wants to bake, a slow burn friends-to-lovers romance, and an adorable baking dragon.
- Speed Dating With The Denizens Of The Underworld (shared world): a paranormal romance shared world based on mythology from around the world. Each book follows a different couple.
- Blackthorn Academy For Supernaturals (shared world): a

paranormal monster romance shared
world based at Blackthorn Academy.
Each book follows a different couple.

You can find a complete list of all my books on my
website:

https://books.authorlauragreenwood.co.uk/book-
list

Signed Paperback & Merchandise:

You can find signed paperbacks, hardcovers, and
merchandise based on my series (including stickers,
magnets, face masks, and more!) via my website:

https://books.authorlauragreenwood.co.uk/shop

About Laura Greenwood

Laura is a USA Today Bestselling Author of paranormal romance, urban fantasy, and fantasy romance. When she's not writing, she drinks a lot of tea, tries to resist French macarons, and works towards a diploma in Egyptology. She lives in the UK, where most of her books are set. Laura specialises in quick reads, with healthy relationships and consent-positive moments regardless of if she's writing light-hearted romance, mythology-heavy urban fantasy, or anything in between.

Follow Laura Greenwood

- Website: www.authorlaura-greenwood.co.uk
- Mailing List: https://books.authorlauragreenwood.co.uk/newsletter

- Facebook Group: http://facebook.com/groups/theparanormalcouncil
- Facebook Page: http://facebook.com/authorlauragreenwood
- Bookbub: https://www.bookbub.com/authors/laura-greenwood

www.ingramcontent.com/pod-product-compliance
Lightning Source LLC
Chambersburg PA
CBHW031750150726
47989CB00006B/2662